Skookum Sal, Birling Gal

Heather Kellerhals-Stewart
Illustrations by Janice Blaine

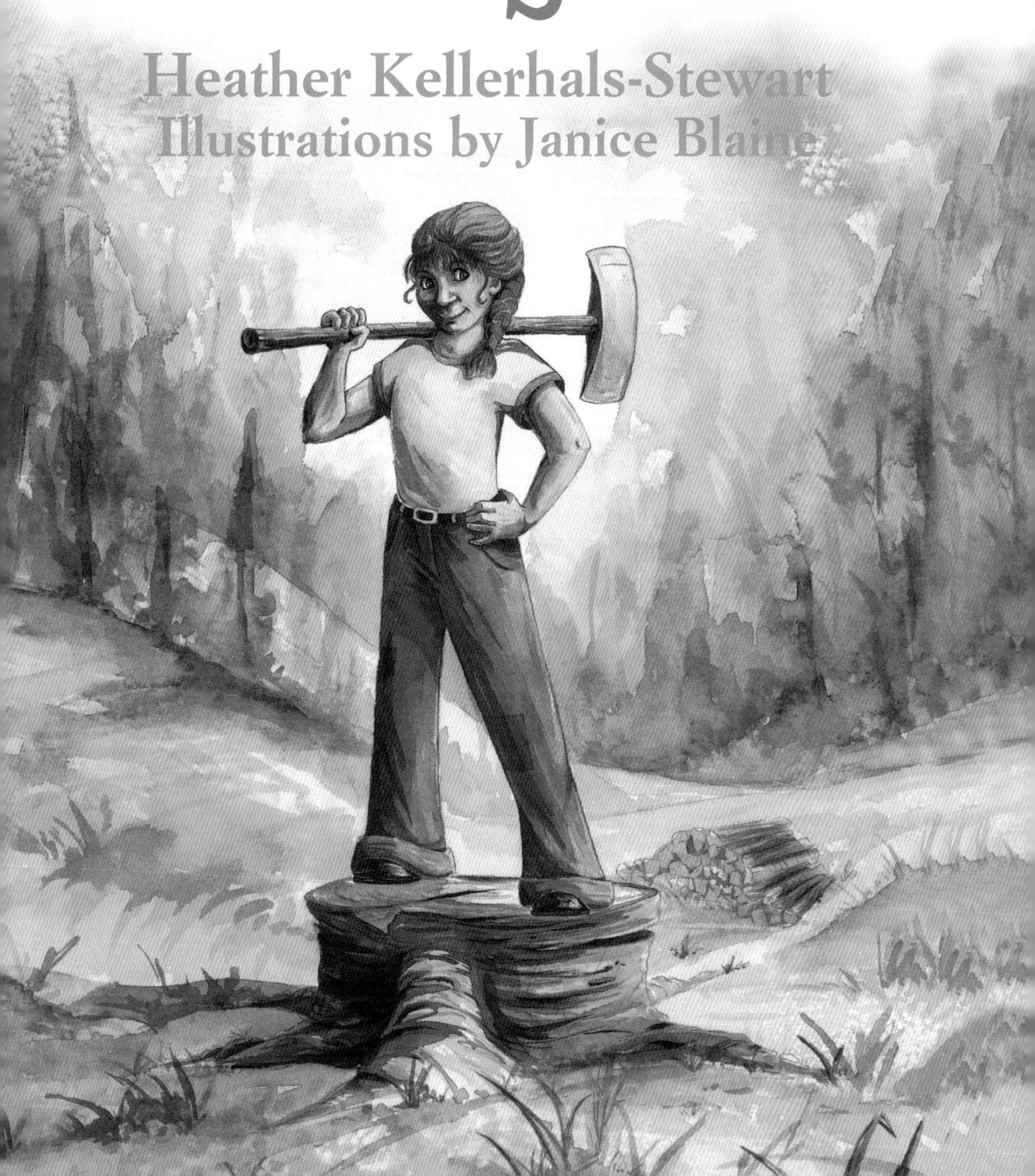

Sal's daddy was a log birler. Her brother Skookum Sam was one too. And long before that her granddaddy and great-granddaddy were log birlers.

At Loggers' Sports Days Sam and his rival would hop atop a floating log and start it rolling or birling like a wheel. Pretty soon one of them would lose his balance and go overboard. And it wasn't Sam. He always won the grand prize.

You might say log birling ran in Sal's family. All over their house were pictures of fleet-footed log birlers, past and present.

It was only fitting for Sal to believe that one day she too would be a world-famous birler. So when Sal was eleven years old she said to her mom, who was up to her ears in spring cleaning, "When do I start?"

"Start what, dear?"

"Log birling, of course."

"Better talk to your daddy. He has the know-how, not me."

"How come you aren't a log birler like Daddy?"

"Not enough time, dear. Too busy spring cleaning."

This didn't sound like much fun, so Sal went outside to talk to her daddy, who was chopping his way through a pile of firewood. He was only too glad to set down his axe for a spell.

"Lovely day," he said, sniffing the air.
"When do I start, Daddy?"
"Start what, sweetie?"

"Log birling, like you and Sam and Granddaddy and Great-Granddaddy..."

"You need more muscle power, Sal. Your brother, Sam, was twelve or more before he started."

"Gals my age are way bigger than boys," Sal pointed out, standing tall.

Her daddy sighed. "True enough, but when did you last see a lady log birler around this neck of the woods?"

Sal flexed her muscles. "Hand me your axe, Daddy, and I'll show you how strong I am."

As he watched, Sal cut and stacked a pile of wood neat and tight as any man could do.

Her daddy sighed again. "You win Sal, there's no denying your muscle power. But there's more to birling than strength."

"Like what?" Sal asked, wiping her brow.

"Like balance, like feet that can dance on a dime and run faster than a deer. And a little craft never hurts."

Sal hopped onto a stump and skipped circles there until her daddy grew dizzy watching.

"You win Sal," he sighed. "And I figure you've got the craft part down pat too."

"Craft means trickery, huh Daddy?"

"Some might call it trickery. I call it out-thinking your opponent. But more of that after we've got you started."

He took Sal's arm and swung her into the air. For a moment she hung there, half thinking she might fly away like a wild goose. But remembering the birling, she was happy to be lowered back down to earth. The moss was soft and steamy and spring-smelling. It was nice lying there, listening to the dew worms rummaging below and the geese honking above.

Sal's daddy put on a stern look. "Well, Sal, if you're serious about this we better quit dawdling and head out to the practice pond."

The pond was full of frogs—a regular opera of croaking. But when they heard Sal and her daddy come striding along, the frogs all hushed up.

Sal's daddy pointed to a slimy old log floating by the shore. "There's the birling log, same one as taught Sam."

"And now it's mine, right Daddy?"

"Right you are, Sal. But before you set off ..."

Sal took a flying leap onto the log. Her legs skittered out from under her. SPLAT! Into the froggy waters went Sal. When she came to the surface, she was spluttering.

"You never told me that log was slithery with frog slime, Daddy."

"Like your ma says, Sal, look before you leap. And listen too."

Sal scowled at him and sprang atop the log again.

Before she knew it that log was rolling 'round and 'round and she was running faster and faster just to keep up until ... SPLAT!

The log won again. This time though, Sal came up smiling.

"Birling is fun, right Daddy?"

"Right you are. But next time keep an eye on that slimy old log. When it goes fast forward, then's the time for you to backpedal. Watch how your daddy does it."

He stepped cautiously onto the log. It lay there sullen-like, as if eyeing him through one knothole. Sal's daddy took a few steps forward. The log rolled under his feet. But Sal's daddy was already running backwards. Pretty soon that log was doing just what he wanted.

"WOW!" was all Sal could say. "Can I do that too, Daddy?"

"Course you can, sweetie. All you need is practice."

And practise Sal did—all spring and part way into summer. One day her brother Skookum Sam dropped by, all decked out in his hard safety hat and caulk boots with sharp spikes on the bottoms for walking on logs.

"Where you heading?" she asked him.

"Logging show, up Island a ways."

"Want to see how good I am?" Sal asked.

"Sure, Sis, fire away."

Well, Sal stepped onto that slimy old log so nice and easy it scarcely moved. With her feet she coaxed it into going backwards or forwards, fast or slow, whatever she wanted. She danced. She twirled on one foot.

"Well?"

Sam took off his hard hat and scratched his head. "Some mighty fancy footwork there."

Sal grinned. "You think I'm good, huh?"

"Not half bad. You aiming to challenge some big, burly logger?"

"Maybe."

"You got a thing or two to learn then." Sam hopped onto the slimy old log with her and stood there steady as a woodpecker clinging to an old snag-tree.

Sal crossed her arms. "What's stalling you, big brother?"

Sam just stood there. Meanwhile, Sal was whistling and looking 'round at the view. With as much warning as a hawk gives before snatching up a chicken, Sam started backpedalling full tilt. Sal didn't stand a chance … SPLAT!

Sam squelched a grin as he helped his sister up. "Caught you off guard, right?" He plucked a lily pad from her head.

"Is that what Daddy means by craft?"

Sam nodded. "You need craft and staying power. And you need caulk boots like mine with nails on the bottom, so's you can stick with your log. I'm aiming to fix you with a pair before I head up coast."

"You sure are one nice brother, Sam."

"Don't mention it, Sis."

With her new caulk boots, Sal practised 'til summer ran into fall and fall into winter. The trouble was having no sparring partner. And where to find one? Sal cast her eyes about until they landed on Flora, the family's pet goose, who was swimming nearby.

A handful of grain lured her onto the slimy old log. 'Round they spun, webbed feet and caulk books—faster and faster until the goose was flying. And SPLAT! Sal was swimming.

"Fowl play," Sal spluttered. "Nobody wins."

All winter they practised birling, except when a cold spell blew down from the northwest and froze the pond. Sal sprawled on the ice staring at the lily pads swaying below. Were the frogs safely tucked into the mud?

Flora stood nearby on one leg. Her feet were freezing too.

"Sal," her mom hollered from the door of the house, "how about splitting some cedar kindling for the stove? That'll warm you up, guaranteed."

Then overnight a warm southeast wind blew in and licked the ice away. Spring began returning with little backward and forward rushes. One day her brother, Skookum Sam, blew in too.

"How's the birling going?" he asked.

"Come down to the pond and see for yourself."

Flora the goose watched as the two stepped onto that slimy old birling log.

Sam smiled at Sal and Sal smiled right back. Sam did a two-step forward and Sal followed. Sam spun and faced the other way and Sal spun too.

SAL

Sam kicked water in her face and Sal kicked water right back. They were both spluttering and laughing.

After a spell Sam got serious and said, "Right ... so now's the time to end this little game."

"Right you are," Sal called back.

Well, Sam started out like some runaway logging truck. Lickety-split he went—faster, slower, now changing gears, now into reverse. And Sal stuck with him until ... her foot hit a knot on that slimy old birling log. She looked to be going overboard when Flora the goose launched an attack on Sam's leg.

"Ow," Sam yelled, clutching his leg as he hit the water.

Flora stood on the log, flapping her wings triumphantly.

"Fair or fowl, you win," Sam said, pulling himself onto dry land. "And you know what, Sal? Loggers' Sports Day is comin' up soon. I'd say you're mighty ready."

"You figure they'll let me birl, Sam? Being a gal and all?"

"Wear a hard hat and no one will know the diff."

"Can you find one that'll fit my head?"

"Sure, Sis … we can tuck that red hair of yours up inside it so nobody will guess you're a gal."

"Thanks Sam."

"Don't mention it," Sam replied, emptying the pond water from his boots.

Right on schedule the Loggers' Sports Day rolled into town. All the different types who work in the woods were hightailing it to the fair grounds—fallers and flunkeys, boom men and bull cooks, high riggers and high climbers, log scalers and cat skinners and chokermen, even a bull of the woods or two.

Sal, her brother Sam and the whole family were heading that way too, in their rattly old pickup truck.

When Sal spied all the big, burly loggers she swallowed hard. “You really figure I’m ready to birl against those burly bruisers, Sam?”

“Why sure, Sis. Drop pretty near any of those loggers atop a birling log and they’d go haywire.”

A noisy man wearing a top hat was bellowing through his bullhorn, “As mayor of Land’s End—salmon capital and fir tree capital of the world—I declare our annual Loggers’ Sports Day OPEN. We may be small, but by gosh our hearts are big. Go to it, boys.”

Well you should have seen the dust rising, the axes chopping, the loggers cussing, the cross-cut saws biting into logs …

You could hear those loggers clear across the border. Ma won the axe throw. Daddy won the tree climbing. And as for Sam, he was winning just about everything he entered.

Sal kept fingering her hard hat. "When's my turn coming up, Sam?"

"Don't get ants in your pants. And keep that hard hat out of sight. That's your disguise."

The day was winding down. Kids were cranky. Hot dog buns, mustard, jellyroll goo, dill pickles, candy floss and popcorn littered the fair grounds.

The noisy man in the top hat was hollering through his bullhorn, “Ladies, gents, loggers and others … the event you’ve all been waiting for—the log birling challenge. Is there anyone out there who dares go against our reigning champ, Big Bear Brown?”

Sam poked his sister. “That’ll be you, Sal.”

Sal watched as a bear of a man with oversized caulk boots strode to the pool’s edge.

“Look at his size!” Sal whispered.

Sam patted her hard hat. “Don’t let the size of that burly bruiser faze you, Sis. Remember what Mom is always saying, the bigger they are, the harder they fall.”

“I’ll go against him,” Sal finally called out.

She stood tall and marched forward, praying her hair would stay tucked inside her hard hat.

The reigning champ growled. “I’m supposed to share the log with this pipsqueak? He’s a regular no-see-um. Ha, ha, ha!”

The crowd laughed too.

He won’t be laughing for long, Sal promised herself.

“Contestants ready? Helpers and everyone else stand back. Let ’er rip.”

After trying to glare Sal down, the burly bruiser started running forward. Clumpety-clump, smackety-smack. His boots were so big they kept hitting the water. Sal ran along beside him, her steps nice and easy, like waves skittering across a pond. The burly bruiser got riled and started running backwards. Clumpety-clump, smackety-smack went the big boots. Sal followed him nice and easy.

"Can't you do nothin' on your own, pipsqueak?" the big man roared.

With one foot Sal splashed water in his face. With the other foot she splashed more water.

"Way to go, kid," the crowd cheered.

The sound infuriated the champ. He shook his head like an angry grizzly and he almost lost his balance.

"You've got him on the run, kid," the crowd roared.

Hearing this, the burly bruiser went berserk. "I can play that game too. Just you watch me."

With his size-thirteen boots he tried to splash Sal, but like big paddles they kept getting stuck underwater.

"Now make a dash for it, kid," the crowd shouted.

Sal started running forward as fast as she could, spinning the log and jumping up and down just to make it bounce. The big bruiser stumbled around, not knowing where the little no-see-um was headed next.

"Use your craft," Sam shouted.

Sal stopped dead in her tracks, twirled and faced her rival. For a minute they glared at each other, saying nothing. The crowd went wild. Then the bear of a man, thinking to catch Sal off guard, lunged forward, spinning the log like it was a measly matchstick. But the quick-footed flyweight was ready for him. As fast as he birled the log, she rolled it faster, until those big grizzly-bear feet got all tangled up. Head first he flew—SPLAT! Some of the bystanders got soaked it was such a humongous splash. Sal leaped from the log and tore off her hard hat.

"And the winner is, SKOOKUM SAL!" Sam shouted, holding up her arm.

Sal's daddy swung her into the air. "I figured that high-stepping gnat was you, Sal. Granddaddy would sure as heck be pleased."

Sal's grin stretched all the way 'round her loose tooth and back again.

“You suppose log birling runs in the family, Daddy?”

“You can say that again,” he said, catching her on the way down.

For Margo Cormack of Page 11 Books in Campbell River, a great supporter of writers and writing. And for Ken Bostock, her late partner—log scaler, adroit log leaper and lover of books and music.

Published by
Harbour Publishing Co. Ltd., P.O. Box 219, Madeira Park, BC V0N 2H0
www.harbourpublishing.com

Cover and page design by Charon O'Brien
Illustrations by Janice Blaine

Printed and bound in China through Colorcraft Ltd., Hong Kong

Harbour Publishing acknowledges financial support from the Government of Canada through the Book Publishing Industry Development Program and the Canada Council for the Arts; and from the Province of British Columbia through the British Columbia Arts Council and the Book Publisher's Tax Credit through the Ministry of Provincial Revenue.

National Library of Canada Cataloguing in Publication Data

Kellerhals-Stewart, Heather, 1937-
Skookum Sal, birling gal / Heather Kellerhals-Stewart ; Janice Blaine, illustrator.

ISBN 1-55017-285-9

I. Title.
PS8571.E447S65 2003 jC813'.54 C2003-911174-1